THINK YOU CAN HANDLE
JAMIE KELLY'S FIRST YEAR OF DIARIES?

#1 LET'S PRETEND THIS NEVER HAPPENED

#2 MY PANTS ARE HAUNTED!

#3 AM I THE PRINCESS OR THE FROG?

#4 NEVER DO ANYTHING, EVER

#5 CAN ADULTS BECOME HUMAN?

#6 THE PROBLEM WITH HERE IS THAT IT'S WHERE I'M FROM

#7 NEVER UNDERESTIMATE YOUR DUMBNESS

#8 IT'S NOT MY FAULT I KNOW EVERYTHING

#9 THAT'S WHAT FRIENDS AREN'T FOR

#10 THE WORST THINGS IN LIFE ARE ALSO FREE

#11 OKAY, SO MAYBE I DO HAVE SUPERPOWERS

#12 ME! (JUST LIKE YOU, ONLY BETTER)

AND DON'T MISS YEAR TWO!

YEAR TWO #1: SCHOOL. HASN'T THIS GONE ON LONG ENOUGH?

YEAR TWO #2: THE SUPER-NICE ARE SUPER-ANNOYING

YEAR TWO #3: NOBODY'S PERFECT. I'M AS CLOSE AS IT GETS.

YEAR TWO #4: WHAT I DON'T KNOW MIGHT HURT ME

DEAR DUMB DIARY,

OKAY, SO MAYBE i DO HAVE SUPERPOWERS

BY JAMIE KELLY

SCHOLASTIC inc.

ISBN 978-0-545-11615-2

20 19 18   18 19 20/0
Printed in the U.S.A.   40
First printing, January 2011

*No actual clowns were harmed in
the making of this diary. Much.*

*Superhuman thanks to Kristen LeClerc
and my Scholastic partners in crime:
Steve Scott, Elizabeth Krych, Susan Jeffers,
Anna Bloom, and Shannon Penney.*

This Diary
Property Of

Jamie Kelly

SCHOOL: Mackerel Middle School

FRIENDS: ISABELLA, EMMILY
STINKETTE, ANGELINE, STINKER

Special Abilities: Writing, Dancing,
Glitterization, Drawing, Ant care

DON'T READ MY DIARY!!

OR MY
ICE VISION
OR SMOKE VISION—
OR STINK VISION
OR BEAGLE VISION

And YES, There IS SUCH A THING AS BEAGLE VISION

SO JUST WATCH IT.

Dear Whoever Is Reading My Dumb Diary,

I command you to stop reading it **NOW**. I am just an average, mild-mannered citizen of this fair city, and there is no reason for you to suspect that I am secretly keeping something about myself a secret.

If you are my parents, I know that I am not allowed to call people names or point out their weaknesses or stuff like that. But I am allowed to write it. And, if you accuse me of doing anything that I've written in this diary, I will know that you read it, which I do **not** give you permission to do.

(Although perhaps you used **mutated mental powers** to read my mind. If so, you're just going to have to knock that off, too.)

All other criminals, villains, misfits, and mutants **be warned**, for I am watching your every move — except gross, private,

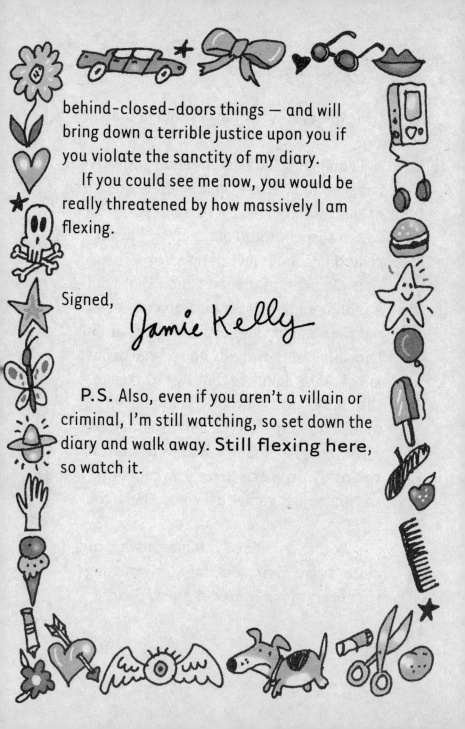

behind-closed-doors things — and will bring down a terrible justice upon you if you violate the sanctity of my diary.

If you could see me now, you would be really threatened by how massively I am flexing.

Signed,

Jamie Kelly

P.S. Also, even if you aren't a villain or criminal, I'm still watching, so set down the diary and walk away. **Still flexing here,** so watch it.

Sunday 01

Dear Dumb Diary,

    If somebody ever asks you to kick her in the face, the first thing she will do is forget that she asked you to do it.

    Isabella was over today, and we were working on my hair. i cut my hair really short over the summer and thought that it might grow back **beautiful** and **luxurious** because that's what would have happened in a fairy tale, and I believe that sooner or later I'm entitled to a fairy tale.

    But it grew in thicker. SO thick, in fact, that I think that maybe each of my hair holes now has two hairs crowding out through the space that used to have only one.

    Angeline also cut her hair really short, and of course hers DID grow back silkier and more spectacular, but I sort of expected that. I'm almost surprised that money didn't grow out of her head as well.

also my hairs seem meaner

We actually had some fun with Angeline over the summer: going to an amusement park, going to the zoo, sitting quietly and listening to her hair grow. (You really can hear it. Her nails, too.)

At some point during the summer, I started to think that it was **wrong** of me to hate Angeline because of how she looked. And smelled. And laughed. And smiled. And blinked. And sat.

When I finally saw past the gorgeousness, when I peered deep into the essence of Angeline, when I tried not to see the cascading waterfall of glimmering blond satin spilling over her shoulders and puddling in the hearts of every boy nearby, I saw a person who was kind, and generous, and honest, and good. And I realized that I shouldn't hate her for her looks.

There's just **so, so, so much more** to hate her for.

HATE the PLEASANTNESS

Hate the FACT SHE's SO HARD TO HATE

HATE THE NICENESS

And yet, I really don't think I **do** hate her anymore. While it's true that she won the looks lottery, and the personality lottery, and the soul lottery, and all of the other lotteries, none of that is really *her* fault.

So, if anything, I suppose I should pity Angeline for being born so hatable.

I know, Dumb Diary. It's hard to understand how excellent that makes me — to *not* hate somebody who seems to be asking for it — but let me clear it up for you: It makes me PURE excellent. As excellent as an angel with the power to shoot frosting out her eyes.

Now, back to my foot and the relationship it recently had with Isabella's face.

We were watching one of those super-stupid superhero movies after we gave up on my hair (there's really nothing to be done), and I noticed that there was a lot of face kicking — like, more than you normally see in a day. So, I commented on how fake it was. I mean: You don't have to *kick* a person's face — if somebody just *stepped* on your face a couple times, you'd go into total meltdown. (I know what I'm talking about: In fourth grade, Isabella saw an ant on my cheek while I was lying on the couch.)

Isabella said that getting kicked in the face isn't that big of a deal and that I could kick her in the face just to prove it, and I said no way I would never do that and then I kicked her in the face anyway, because I guess I **changed my mind** really quick.

Minds are so silly.

my adorable / fiendish mind

Isabella stayed on the floor for about five minutes saying things that probably could only be understood by others recently kicked in the face. I explained what happened and helped her up. In her daze, she didn't believe that she had asked me to kick her, but mostly she didn't believe that I had **done** it.

Fortunately, I've watched a lot of crime shows and so provided a smear of her lip balm on the bottom of my sock as evidence. (Also, I pointed out that her glasses were on top of the bookshelf.)

Isabella was having a hard time with this, because her mean older brothers have made her into a good fighter. She couldn't accept that a **"huge, girly, sissy girl"** like me could ever land a kick on her.

I guess this is
How Isabella
sees me

french
poodle

french
fanciness

french
umbrella
you carry
when you
know it's
not going
to rain

Later on, as I was wiping her saliva off a wall, I apologized, but Isabella still seemed a little dazed. I feel bad now, but I think I proved my point about how dumb superhero movies are — and in particular, how much more significant **face-kickery** actually is than it seems in movies.

Monday 02

Dear Dumb Diary,

So they're still making me do science even though I have been helpfully pointing out for years that nobody really needs it.

Seriously, the scientists we already have seem to have it under control. I can't imagine them wanting me to walk into the lab and start fiddling around with some big bowl of electrons they had out.

Wouldn't it be simpler just to *tell* the scientists what we want them to discover, and leave it to them to figure it out? We don't have to *invent food* when we go to restaurants; we just tell waitresses what we want and they bring it. Seems like this should work for science as well.

Besides, scientists already have their lab coats and accessories and everything.

My new science teacher, Mrs. Maple — who is always in a bad mood and likes to wear sandals so that we may observe that her third toes are, like, two inches longer than her big toes and are, therefore, medically considered to be fingers — doesn't see it this way, of course. She is making me do science anyway. Right now we're studying ants, which might sound boring, but let me assure you, it's really a lot less interesting than boring.

It turns out that ants have all kinds of **complex** and **highly sophisticated** features that have developed over millions and millions of years but can't keep them from getting stepped on by a five-year-old, in spite of the fact that everybody who sees a five-year-old studying an ant knows what's coming next.

It's kind of amazing that nobody in Antworld ever predicted the trouble that a size-two shoe was going to present. Seems like maybe it's the ants that need some scientists.

It was during the most fascinating part of the lesson about ants that Isabella **woke me up** with a nudge between my shoulder blades.

She whispered, "You could never kick me in the face like that again."

Isabella must have been thinking about this all night. After many years, I know that whenever Isabella thinks about something too long, there's going to be trouble. (Though if she doesn't think about something long enough, it can go badly, too.) I blatantly tried to change the subject by saying, "The **Fun Fair** is coming."

SOMETIMES IT'S BEST TO DISRUPT
The thoughts of the Schemey

9

The stupidly named Fun Fair is a big fundraiser for our school. They set up games where you can win prizes and there's a big auction of stuff that people donate.

Isabella loves the Fun Fair because a lot of the games involve throwing things at other things, which is one of the **Destructive Arts**, and Isabella is an expert in them all. The Destructive Arts are exactly like Martial Arts, except they don't have uniforms or usefulness and the end result doesn't resemble art in any way.

Of course, we are too sophisticated to *officially* enjoy the Fun Fair. But I've learned that as long as you keep laughing at how dumb something is, you can secretly enjoy it without risking your cool.

It's so Dumb how we're playing with these DoLLs.

Yeah. It's been Dumb for the Last two HOURS.

When she noticed us whispering, Mrs. Maple gave me a mean look that I knew was meant to say, *Be quiet or I'll walk over there with my elongated toes and maybe one of them will brush up against you and how would you like that?*

She may not have meant to mention her elongated toes in this look, but if somebody has mutated third toes that are two inches longer than their big toes, that threat is always implied. **Always.**

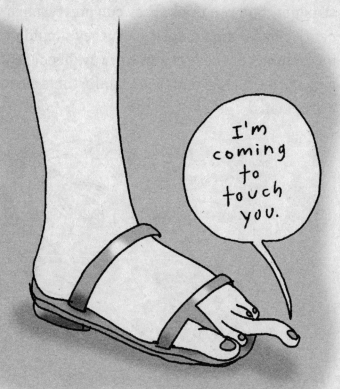

After class, Isabella was talking to Angeline about the Fun Fair, and how last year I made them stop doing the game where you pop balloons with darts.

I hadn't really meant to make them stop. It's just that I got a little wild with a toss and it landed in Beepo's nose.

I had to point out — for her information — that this is actually **precisely** why clowns wear those protective fake noses. And by the way, they're stronger than you think: They can pretty much very nearly almost stop a dart. Plus, they shouldn't even have clowns at these things anyway, because they make some people a little uncomfortable since they are demons.

A CLOWN SHRIEK IS LESS COMICAL THAN YOU MIGHT THINK

The two of them were cackling pretty hard, and Angeline said that she was sure that I couldn't be **THAT** bad at those fair games.

This made Isabella laugh harder and explain that I was so rattled by the clown's screams that my second dart — which I really think would have missed Beepo if he hadn't flinched so bad — stuck in his palm when he put up his large, comical gloves to protect his face.

Angeline correctly pointed out that these were just two accidents that could have happened to anybody, and the clown really wasn't hurt due to his protective clown attire. Isabella agreed but gasped, between howls of laughter, "Jamie had *three* darts."

I don't want to talk about the third dart. While it's true that **Dart Number Three** is probably the main reason they banned the game at our school and most schools in the state, and why the hospital actually has an official procedure now called the **Third Dartectomy**, I feel that I'm much better at those games now. (I've heard Beepo feels much better now, too.)

Angeline said that she was sure I was every bit as good as Isabella at the games, and Isabella's eyes flashed first with a terrible anger, and then with an immeasurable joy.

"Okay, we'll have a contest at the Fun Fair, Jamie. You and I will play the bottle-toss game. And whoever loses," Isabella said slowly as she tried to concoct a suitable penalty, "has to take a one-minute inhale of the inside of Mike Pinsetti's locker."

"No," Angeline whispered deviously. **"Loser has to kiss him."**

Disturbing.

Isn't it?

14

This caused a stomachache to ripple through all three of us, and possibly through all females in the universe. Honestly, when she drops him off at school, even Pinsetti's mom just shakes his hand.

I knew that anything that involved kissing Pinsetti had **BAD IDEA** written all over it. And it was written in pimple medicine.

"Deal," Isabella said.

"Deal," Angeline said.

"Wait!" I said.

But nobody waited, and I guess I made a deal.

15

Tuesday 03

Dear Dumb Diary,

I didn't sleep well last night. I kept thinking about how, in just a few weeks, I will probably be boiling my lips. That is the only way to remove the **Pinsetti stain** that's going to be left there.

At school, I pointed out to Isabella that Angeline made this deal for the both of us, but that Angeline is the only one with nothing to lose.

"I don't have anything to lose, either," Isabella said. "Because I'm going to win."

I asked her to **please please please** let me out of the deal, but she said no. I told her it wasn't fair because my arm still hurt where Fat Ricky bit me so I wouldn't be able to throw at the bottle toss. Plus, I used three pleases.

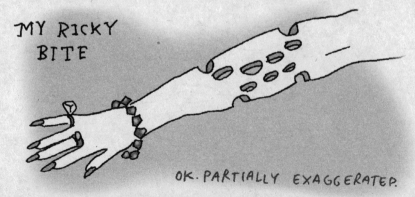

MY RICKY BITE

OK. PARTIALLY EXAGGERATED.

Let me explain: **Fat Ricky** is this little kid that Angeline babysits sometimes. Isabella and I stopped by her house last Thursday.

When we opened the door, Angeline was holding Fat Ricky, and when he spotted Isabella, he lunged at her. (Babies instinctively hate her.) Isabella dodged as nimbly as a bullfighter, because it was pretty much your standard biting lunge and her brothers try that on her all the time.

I was standing directly behind Isabella, and so Fat Ricky bit me right on the arm. And trust me, even though babies don't have all their teeth, the few they do have are like little weasel teeth and they hurt like crazy. This is why scientists are always telling us: **Avoid baby bites.** (Or they *should* tell us that anyway.)

MUNCH

BABY WOUNDS are most similar to those scientists see in Walrus Maulings

Isabella's eyes popped open wide and she repeated it: "That's right. He *bit* you."

This isn't how Isabella typically reacts to a person being bitten. Usually, she just laughs because generally, it's her doing the biting.

"That explains it," she said.

She pulled me to the side and explained in a whisper that Fat Ricky is probably radioactive, which would explain why everyone handles his diapers that way. (Arm's length; brisk run to the trash.)

Isabella said that when Ricky bit me, my DNA was somehow transformed, the same way that superheroes are always getting their DNA transformed. She says that I now have the superpowers of **Being Like a Boy**, and that explains how I managed to kick her, because a big sissy girl like me could never do it with my regular old sissy-girl powers.

Let's be more careful not to get mutated, folks

-CAUTION-
DANGEROUS
MYSTERY
RAY
DEVICE

18

I told her that this sounded like a fairy tale. In fact, all of the superhero stories sound like fairy tales, with big, strong weight lifters in long underwear filling in for the fairy princesses.

Superheroes—SERIOUSLY. would it KILL YOU to wear regular clothes to WORK?

"Maybe," Isabella said quietly, "but don't you believe that sooner or later you're entitled to a fairy tale?"

While it was clear that Isabella had obviously been reading my diary (STOP IT NOW, ISABELLA), I also thought that maybe she really and truly believed this stuff. And if so, it might get me out of the whole bottle toss—Pinsetti kiss thing.

"So," I said. "The bet's off, right? Since I have powers now?"

Isabella thought about this for a full minute, which is enough time for Isabella to think pretty hard. Some of Isabella's most dangerous thoughts come in at around sixty seconds.

"Nope," she said. **"The bet stands."**

"But what about my superpowers?" I said. To make the point, I struck a pose like a superhero. I've noticed that they always seem to have time to pose in spite of all the bad guys running around.

She said she didn't care, and I had to believe her. If there is one thing Isabella excels at, it's carelessness.

Things Isabella Wouldn't Care About:

Titanic sinking Again.

Meteor striking Earth and landing directly on top of World's most innocent panda.

Titanic sinking again and this time the entire crew is puppies.

Wednesday 04

Dear Dumb Diary,

There's a lot of talk going around about the fair, and it sounds like some of the boys are actually asking some of the girls to **meet up with them there**. These aren't dates, exactly, not in the grossest sense of the word. But the idea is to meet at the Fun Fair and then hang around together, and I suppose the boys try to win you a prize because boys are just man-puppies, and men will work much harder to win a prize for a girl than they ever would for themselves.

man-puppies

Wait. One. Second.

How did I know that? Is it possible that I really am developing the superpowers of a boy? Is it possible that I'm beginning to understand the workings of their twisted, damaged, cloudy, disturbed, and occasionally adorable minds?

I have to concentrate. Let me see if I can understand why they would want to watch sports on TV all day. . . .

Nope. I have no idea, and I thought in such a **manly way** that I almost accidentally grew a mustache.

Isabella is wrong. There's no such thing as superpowers.

(Although I am not fully prepared to give up on fairy tales.)

Especially MY VERSIONS

Red Riding Hood tames wolf. Teaches it to eat her teachers.

Handsome Prince SO NOT impressed with Cinderella's Beauty. Chooses her brunette friend instead.

OLD LADY WHO LIVED IN A SHOE moves to the Beach and lives in a flip-flop.

Thursday 05

Dear Dumb Diary,

    Thursday is always Meat Loaf Day at our school.

    There are two questions I believe the entire world is asking: How can the world not have run out of meat loaf by now, and what the heck is it made of?

    They serve it to us at school every week, they're serving it at other schools, and regular people are even eating it at home for dinner. (Don't ask me why.) Doesn't it seem that our meat loaf mines should be depleted by now?

    And think about it: If we have so much meat loaf, isn't there something more sensible we can do with it instead of eating it?

    I ask Miss Bruntford, the cafeteria monitor, what it's made of almost every week, and I've kept track of her most common answers:

Today, the **suffocating, rank pew** of the meat loaf was astonishing, but it did not diminish the spirits of the jillion boys that kept wandering up to our table to ask Angeline if she would hang out with them at the Fun Fair. I think that bad odors really do not bother males that much, and it is mainly for this reason that they can stand to be around themselves.

After each boy asked, Angeline just smiled and politely said no thanks, and we watched the boys emotionally **crackle** and **fizzle** like little insects that had been drawn into a blond bug light.

The weird thing is that it seemed like all the boys, even the ones who were clearly way too low on the popularity totem pole, felt entitled to ask Angeline, who is close to the very top. (**Please note:** There actually *is* a popularity totem pole. I made it.)

Like, if you were some kind of spindly little goat, would you ask a gazelle to go for a gallop? No, of course not. You wouldn't be qualified. You would ask a she-goat or a tortoise, or — what are those things with the wrinkly skin and sad eyes? — oh yeah, your grandma.

But for some reason, boys just aren't **appropriately intimidated** by Angeline.

Except maybe for Hudson Rivers (eighth cutest boy in my school. I may have mentioned him before. Future husband or future ex-husband, haven't decided). Angeline told me that he's just about the only one who hasn't asked her.

See, here's the thing with Hudson: I'm pretty sure that Angeline has a crush on him, and I'm sure he has one on her, too, because — let's be honest here — all human males do. He's had a crush on Isabella, but Isabella isn't interested in him because of Isabella's well-known policy of dealing with feelings of this nature. (She doesn't.)

Hudson probably knows that I have had a crush on him, and he might have had one on me at one time, but because of all of this twisted history, he doesn't want to create any problems between three friends (even though Angeline is more friends with us than we are with her).

So what.
It just means
that MALE
GERMS are more
attracted to her.

27

Wait. One. Second.

How weird is it that I **TOTALLY KNOW WHAT HE'S FEELING?**

Perhaps I must just accept that boy DNA is actually fusing with my own nicer, prettier DNA.

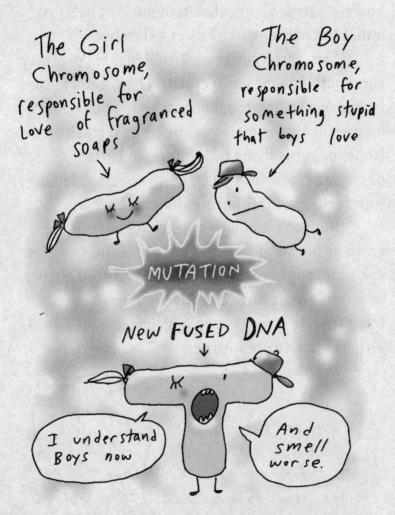

The Girl Chromosome, responsible for Love of fragranced soaps

The Boy Chromosome, responsible for something stupid that boys love

MUTATION

New FUSED DNA

I understand Boys now

And smell worse.

Friday 06

Dear Dumb Diary,

Today, Isabella asked us who the best athletes at our school were. I had no idea, and couldn't figure out why Isabella even cared. But I was distracted when Angeline began spouting off statistics like she was Google.

It turns out that boys like to tell Angeline how good they are at sports. They do it so often that Angeline has a lot of the information memorized, even though she says she has no idea what most of it means. (Which suggests that sports are sort of like many of my favorite songs.)

Isabella actually began **taking notes**, which I believe are the only things I've never seen Isabella take before.

SHE'S TAKEN

A bath   my lunch   Her Sweet time

The Toe (Mrs. Maple) gave us an assignment about ants on Tuesday, and she made Emmily, Isabella, and me partners. The Toe likes to give group projects because it means fewer papers to grade and more time to carefully groom and preen her precious appendages.

I'm sure you recall, Dumb Diary, that Emmily is our friend that spells her name with two m's because it reminds her of candy. For a long time, I thought she meant that it reminded her of candy because of the little m's they print on some candies, but she told me it's really because *mm* is the sound she makes when she eats them. (She thought the letters on the candies were w's anyway.)

And some of them are "three"s.

We need to write a paper *and* have some sort of visual aid for our project, like an ant sculpture, or an ant costume, or something.

What this all means is that Isabella won't help much with the report because reports aren't her thing, and Emmily can't help much because of her micro-brain, so I'll have to single-handedly do a report about an insect that isn't as pretty as a butterfly, or as considerate as a bee — which at least is decent enough to die from guilt after it stings you.

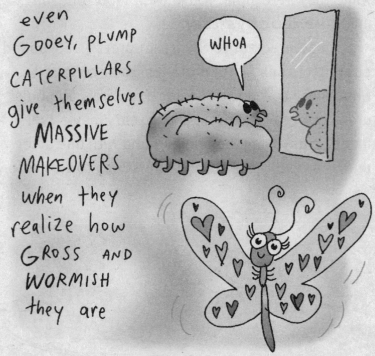

even Gooey, plump caterpillars give themselves MASSIVE MAKEOVERS when they realize how GROSS AND WORMISH they are

Saturday 07

Dear Dumb Diary,

Mom and Dad went out for a fancy dinner tonight, and since Stinker — my bucket of beagle guts — and his dogdaughter, Stinkette, would not be courageous enough to protect me from a psychotic-maniac-vampire-cannibal, they asked my Aunt Carol to come over and hang out with me while they were gone. You know, to look out for me. *Like a babysitter.*

I pointed out to them that pretty, 130-pound babysitters like Aunt Carol seem to be *exactly* what those psychotic-maniac-vampire-cannibals are attracted to in every single scary movie ever made. If anything, hanging around with one after dark is probably the absolute worst way to stay safe.

But they insisted, and I really didn't complain much because I suddenly realized that Aunt Carol is **slower** than I am. This means I don't have to run faster than the psychotic-maniac-vampire-cannibal, I just have to run faster than whoever is with me when the psychotic-maniac-vampire-cannibal starts chasing us.

ALWAYS REMEMBER TO BE THE FASTEST PERSON IN YOUR CROWD

AND BE ABLE TO NOT LOOK DELICIOUS WHENEVER NECESSARY

↑ LOOKING NOT DELICIOUS ON PURPOSE

Dad, as always, was ready for dinner forty minutes before Mom. He sat uncomfortably on the couch impatiently fumbling with the car keys and staring at his watch every couple of minutes, as if looking at it **meanly** might make Mom move quicker.

I knew what he was thinking, and felt I had to explain everything to him.

"Dad," I said, "when you get ready to go out, you shower, maybe shave, and put on clean clothes. At the end of all that, what we have is a man that smells **slightly better** than when the process began."

Dad looked at me and nodded.

"Mom, on the other hand, is totally transformed into a different human being by this process. Not only does she emerge immaculately cleaned and combed, things are colored, perfumed, moisturized, and manipulated in ways you just can't begin to imagine. That kind of **intense lady-magic** just takes longer."

My dad cocked his head in the way that beagles do when they are trying hard to understand something.

He set his keys on the table, leaned back, and smiled. His impatience dissolved away. When Mom came out, he gave her a big hug and off they went.

And as Aunt Carol and I waved good-bye to them, I realized that I had successfully calmed Dad's butt down, and there was only one startling explanation: I must have spoken **The Male Language**.

☆ LADY MOM'S MAGIC ☆

Before   *After*

It gets weirder.

Later on, as Aunt Carol and I watched TV, we started talking. She complained about this friend of hers and how her friend said this one thing about some stuff that made Aunt Carol bring up some junk about this other thing, and before she knew it, they were all like **RAWR RAWR RAWR** at each other.

Of course this all made perfect sense to me, but she said that when she told Uncle Dan (her husband and my assistant principal) the exact same story, he started giving her advice about all kinds of different ways to handle her friend, and **blah blah blah,** and what's even up with that?

This makes perfect sense to all members of GIRLKIND

And it happened again. I understood **The Male Language**.

I told Aunt Carol that I thought when you tell a male about a problem, he will often assume that you want him to **solve the problem**. When you tell a female about a problem, she will often assume that you just want to express how you feel about the problem. Unless you make it clear to the listener that you're looking for something other than what comes naturally to them, that's how it's probably going to go down.

(I even said that exact thing, "That's how it's going to go down," because that's how dudes talk. I think my male superpower made me say it that way.)

Aunt Carol looked at me with her giant, amazed eyes and said, "Huh." Which, because I still speak **The Female Language**, I recognized as meaning: "Oh my gosh. You're right. I never saw it that way before. You are totally right, and pretty, too."

Maybe Isabella was onto something. Maybe superpowers **ARE** real, and maybe I **have some**.

Sunday 08

Dear Dumb Diary,

Isabella and Emmily came over today to work on our science project. I hadn't written down when it was due, and my partners were no help since Isabella said **"never"** and Emmily didn't remember being assigned anything at all.

Or the teacher who assigned it.

Or where her classroom was.

I probably should have felt dumb calling Angeline to ask her, but I did it anyway. She had the date, plus all the details of the assignment, and a book about ants that she offered to lend us.

Angeline was at my house fifteen minutes later. She said she would have been there sooner, but she stopped to catch us a jar full of ants for our visual aid.

Oh. Yay. A whole jar of boring.

While she was patiently answering Emmily's question about why ants don't wear clothes, I was filled with this bizarre regret that Angeline wasn't in our group.

I thought about suggesting that she ask The Toe if she could switch into our group, and then it suddenly occurred to me: **KRYPTONITE.**

My Superpowers of Boyishness have come with a **super-weakness.** Just like Superman is vulnerable to Kryptonite, my boy powers have made me weak and vulnerable in the way that Angeline makes **ALL** boys weak and vulnerable.

If I had made the mistake of asking her to switch into our group, she could have said no, and I would have crackled and fizzled away like the boys that asked her to meet them at the fair.

These powers of mine. Perhaps they come with risks.

like BUGS, if I start flying

Monday 09

Dear Dumb Diary,

I didn't know what to feed the little jar of ants that Angeline brought us. I took a guess and gave them a little piece of my toast and left the radio on so they wouldn't be so bored all day, because I suspect that learning about ants is only about half as boring as being one:

Ant 1: So, uh, do you ever worry that your itsy little neck is just going to snap under the weight of your head?

Ant 2: Stop asking me that. You ask me that, like, every five minutes.

Ant 1: Sometimes I notice my antennae out of the corner of my eye and I'm all, like: AHH! Something is on me! Get it off! Get it off!

Ant 2: Yeah. The antennae again. Listen, I just remembered, I have to go wander around aimlessly now.

Today at school I saw Hudson Rivers (still the eighth cutest boy in my grade), and I attempted to sense what he was feeling with my superpowers. I may have unintentionally struck a bit of a **Sensing Pose**, because he walked right over and asked me what the heck I was doing.

VARIOUS SENSING POSES

I was pretty embarrassed that Hudson caught me sensing him. I'm not sure what the rules are for using your superpowers, but sensing somebody right out there in public might be kind of rude.

"Nothing," I said, which is what you say when you mean **"something,"** which is pretty stupid, I guess. Everybody knows that's exactly what "nothing" means.

Hidden Meanings We All Know

WHAT IS SAID	WHAT IS MEANT
"Maybe."	"Absolutely not."
"I promise."	"I want you to believe this is a promise."
"You can hardly even notice that pimple on your chin."	"For a second I thought you were eating a plum."

Hudson looked at me and grinned. I tried to sense him secretly, but Pinsetti walked past, publicly scratching himself with an enthusiasm and lack of modesty that you rarely see outside of the zoo. The image was so **horrific** that I could think of nothing other than washing my eyeballs.

I can't lose that bet.

By the time I came to my senses again it was time to go to class, and Hudson had walked away.

The Monkeys at the Zoo requested Pinsetti be BANNED due to his OFFENSIVE HYGIENE.

In science, Mrs. Maple told us more about ants and how strong they are. They can lift twenty times their own body weight. If I was as strong as an ant, I suppose that means I could lift a piano.

If I could do that, I would only do it so that I could drop it on the rest of the ants in my colony, because the one thing I'm really learning about ants is that I **don't like them.**

Isabella took notes again, but this time, she took them in class, which is the **fourth weirdest** thing I've ever seen her do in class.

THE 3 WEIRDEST THINGS SHE'S DONE

One time in second grade, she politely paid attention in class.

Briefly colored neatly once.

Now that I think about it, that polite kid was a boy she forced to impersonate her when we had a substitute.

Tuesday 10

Dear Dumb Diary,

Isabella made Angeline go with her to watch basketball practice after school today. Angeline begged me to go along, and Emmily couldn't remember which bus she was supposed to ride home, so she went, too.

Isabella and I had never been to a basketball game at our school, much less a practice. It turns out that basketball is this sport that involves a lot of running and jumping and throwing. The most you can hope for per shot is three points, although it is usually just two. Frankly, I would find two points a little **insulting** after all that effort.

But my superpowers told me that the boys were actually quite thrilled with their measly two points. This was both adorable and sad, like when a baby is thrilled if you give it half a cracker that's been on the floor.

Total DUMB-Headed glee

Isabella watched the practice very carefully, and I thought I saw her taking notes, but that had to have been my imagination. Every once in a while she would tell Angeline to stand up and cheer, and when she did, the boys would play extra hard. I realized (**thanks, superpowers**) it was because they wanted to impress Angeline.

Angeline didn't really seem impressed. I'm sure she was just doing it to make Isabella happy. But the whole thing was really entertaining Emmily, who had to be asked three times to give back the ball and stay off the court.

My mom gave everybody a ride home. Just before Isabella got out of the car, she said that she had some posters I had to help her make. She gave me the rough draft she had scribbled on a piece of paper:

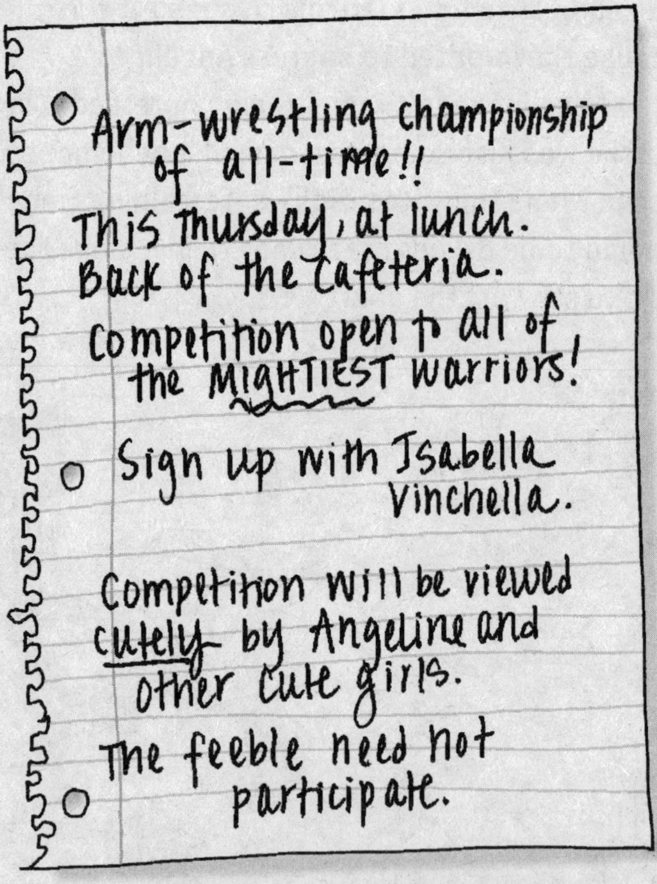

Arm-wrestling championship of all-time!!
This Thursday, at lunch.
Back of the cafeteria.
Competition open to all of the MIGHTIEST warriors!

Sign up with Isabella Vinchella.

Competition will be viewed cutely by Angeline and other cute girls.

The feeble need not participate.

She explained that all she needed me to do was make a couple posters . . .

. . . and get Angeline to come. And come up with some kind of prize. And try to be cute on Friday. (Isabella had observed that girl cuteness seemed to make the basketball players try harder.)

"Or at least, be *cuter,*" she added, to nicely take some of the pressure off. You see, World? Isabella *can* be nice when she wants to be.

Emmily wanted to help with the posters — she's understandably amazed by my glitter abilities — but I told her this looked like a rush job, and I wouldn't be able to train her correctly under this sort of pressure.

Later on, after something that Mom referred to as "dinner," I told my dad about the basketball practice.

He was very interested and even said he'd take me to a real professional game if I wanted to go. (**I didn't.**) He put his arm around me and we watched some other sport on TV together, maybe soccer or baseball? It had some guys running around doing something and some other guys trying to keep them from doing it. That's football, right? Or is that all of them?

I concentrated, and I think I **very nearly** understood why dudes want to watch this stuff so much. My powers are increasing, but I still couldn't quite get it.

But I **HAVE** noticed that DUDES have a Beagley tendency to chase balls.

Wednesday 11

Dear Dumb Diary,

Oh. Some of the ants in our jar found themselves so boring that they died from it. I didn't want to try to take the dead ones out, because they all seem pretty grouchy and I think if I don't draw attention to the dead ones, maybe the live ones won't notice, since the dead ones don't really look any different.

It's probably a source of **great embarrassment** in the ant world when you're talking to a friend for a while and then you notice they're dead, and all the other ants start laughing at you.

Before I left for school, I fed the ants some leaves and Cap'n Crunch, but they didn't seem as interested in eating the stuff as they were in dodging it as it crashed down around them.

I suppose this would be like somebody dropping a sugar-frosted van on me from an airplane, and I made a note for our report about what an unpleasant breakfast experience this would be.

Before I left, I put the ants in front of the TV, hoping they would enjoy that more than the radio, and I gently encouraged them to **die less**.

Emmily helped me and Isabella put up the arm-wrestling posters in the hallway at school. When Angeline saw them, she was **really, really angry** that Isabella had used her name on the poster without asking her first. I'm telling you, the gorgeous of the world can actually look pretty intimidating when they **scowl**. Imagine a snow-white swan with a scary tattoo holding a chain saw. There's just no way to really prepare for that.

Besides the crime of being prettier than those that deserve prettiness more than she does, it's true that we've never actually seen Angeline do anything mean. But like I said, you're never prepared for the chain-saw swan, and Isabella's natural, perfectly normal response to being blamed for something (which is to **fist-fight**) was replaced by the response she usually reserves for times when the other person is much bigger, or a policeman.

She just lied.

Emmily is obviously the least able to defend herself, so Isabella blamed Emmily.

Emmily was somewhat surprised to learn that the Arm-Wrestling Championship had all been her idea, and she started freaking out and squealing saying that it was going to be so much fun, and that it was the best idea she ever had.

I'm pretty sure I saw a little smile try to squirm out from underneath Angeline's chain saw—swan scowl.

Freaking out is **exhausting**, even for full-time freaks, and eventually Emmily ran out of energy. But by then, her enthusiasm had us all looking forward to Isabella's arm-wrestling competition, even Angeline.

A full Aerobic Freak-out includes:

5 minutes of LEGGY-WEGGYS

2 minutes OF RABID ORANGUTAN

And at least 1 "OMG ARE YOU OKAY?"

Thursday 12

Dear Dumb Diary,

    I don't think any more of the ants died, but I can't be sure because I forgot to count them, and when they're all moving around it gets pretty difficult to tell which ants I've already counted.

    I had the great idea of using markers to gently color the ants so I could tell them apart, but I learned that this is exactly like somebody trying to gently color on you with a thirty-story building. Without dwelling on tragedy, I'd just like to say that I'm **deeply sorry** to Mr. Purple and the surviving Purple family.

    I made a note of this in the report, although I did skip over the details of flicking Mr. Purple off the tip of the marker, you know, because it seemed a bit **undignified.**

FLICK

PEWW*

One of the world's worst funerals

I actually heard people talking about the arm-wrestling event this morning, and it was hard to believe that my posters had done such a great job of getting people psyched about something so weird. It was like I was one of those **tremendously talented** people that make great commercials for awful movies.

THE DAY THEY INVENTED PRUNES

NON-START ACTION!

BORING

The Story nobody understood

NOTHING BUT PILGRIMS TALKING

FOR LIKE 2 HOURS

MATH

But by lunch, when we were ready to begin the competition, I realized that it had not been my posters that did the job. It was Emmily that had everybody all wound up.

This wasn't hard to figure out. First, Emmily had given everybody the impression that arm wrestling was an **Olympic event**. (Emmily loves the Olympics. The rings remind her of pancakes, another favorite of hers.) And second, somewhere along the line, Emmily determined that first prize was a **horse**.

Emmily's mistakes didn't hinder Isabella at all. (Few things can. I've seen her hindered, like, twice in her life.) Isabella started setting up the arm wrestlers. She ran the competitions two at a time, with the winner from each competition arm wrestling the winner from the other.

I made sure to watch cutely and cheer. Angeline did, too, although she only had her cute turned up to about a three. (It goes up to **eleven**.)

I have to admit that Angeline did a good job getting this whole thing approved by the principal, which is something Isabella almost never remembers/cares to do.

And as cute as Angeline and I were, Emmily might have been the cutest of all, even though she's usually not terribly cute. (**In her defense:** Shirts really look their best when you don't wear them backward, and Emmily says dressing in the mirror gets her all confused about left and right and inside out.)

Something about her enthusiasm just gets to people.

Emmily could even affect those Dogs that are sad all the time, and the elderly.

The final match came down to Mike Pinsetti and Jake Baker. Jake is in our grade, but he's easily the biggest kid in our school. He's about as wide as he is tall.

Everybody always assumes that big, strong guys like Jake are dumb, but if you thought that about Jake, you'd be wrong. Jake could go to college for ten years and he **still** wouldn't be smart enough to be classified as "**dumb.**"

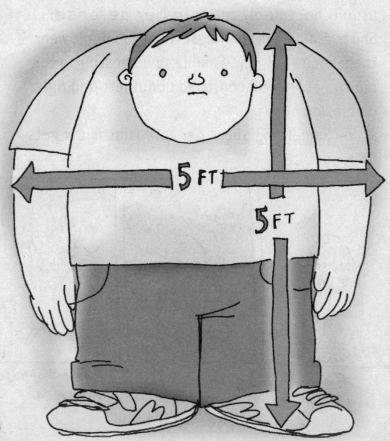

Pinsetti's hand disappeared inside the fleshy folds of Jake's. Emmily, unable to contain herself, let out this ear-piercing cheer that brought a peculiar dumb smile to Jake's dumb face.

Isabella said, **"Go,"** Jake slammed Pinsetti's hand to the table, and everybody cheered — except for Pinsetti, who was making this thin, wheezy pain whine as he stood up and stumbled to the nurse's office to see if somebody there could reassemble the bones in his hand.

Isabella patted Jake on the back and smiled broadly until he turned to her and asked, in a voice that sounded like a garbage disposal full of raw meat:

"Where's my prize? Where's my horse?"

You DO NOT want to fall in there →

But Jake was just asking a place in the air where Isabella *used to be*.

Isabella knew the same thing about psychotic-maniac-vampire-cannibals that I did. In fact, Isabella probably taught me. You don't have to be able to outrun them, you just have to be able to outrun whoever you're with.

And Isabella was with *us*.

Angeline quickly turned her cute up to about a seven, causing anybody directly in front of her face to feel a mild, but pleasant, burning sensation. She smiled at Jake and said, "Yeah. You see, about that horse . . ."

But Jake **wasn't affected**. "Where's my horse?" he said again.

Angeline turned it up to a nine, but he was unaffected. It was like he was throwing Kryptonite all over Angeline's cuteness. He stood up and started looking around for Isabella, like how you might imagine a Tyrannosaurus would look around for a caramel-covered lamb.

NO EFFECT!

And my superpower **tingled**. That's what they do, right? Or do they **jingle**? My superpower **wiggled**. I don't know. But I felt something.

"You haven't beaten everybody yet," I said.

Angeline looked over at me and gritted her teeth.

I steered Emmily to the seat opposite Jake.

"You still have to beat Emmily," I said.

"Yay!" Emmily cheered, unaware that there was a real chance she could be going home with her detached arm in a cooler full of ice.

Emmily put her teeny hand up, and Jake grasped it. As he did, Jake's face became softer and pinker, and he **giggled**. He giggled like a puppy being tickled by a kitten wearing a duckling costume.

It's one of the Giggliest Giggles Known

I said, "Go!" and Emmily strained against his giant ham of an arm. Jake started giggling so hard he began to shake. This made Emmily giggle, and he let her slowly push his hand down to the table.

"**Emmily wins!**" Angeline shouted, and everybody clapped — nobody harder than Jake. I was proud of myself for sensing that Jake's anger would be calmed by Emmily's **Emmilishness**.

But I had neglected to consider one thing.

It was that thing where guys will work way harder to win a prize for a girl than they ever would for themselves.

"WHERE'S HER HORSE?" Jake shouted, now a million times louder and angrier than before. This time, his shouts were directed at the place where Angeline used to be standing.

Now that Isabella and Angeline had both bailed, there was only one victim left. Jake stared at me and snorted and my superpowers told me that there was a chance that somebody was going to get **punched in half** at any moment.

And that's when Angeline dragged Bruntford up to the table. She slid a plate of cafeteria meat loaf in front of Emmily.

"There's your horse," Bruntford said.

We all went silent. We had always suspected that the meat loaf was made of something like that, but was she telling the truth? Or was Bruntford just saying it to quiet everyone down?

"Horsey!" Emmily said and took a big bite. She offered the next one to Jake, who took it with a dumb, sweet smile.

Everybody walked away, and left the **two adorable dopes** to enjoy their repulsive lunch in peace.

On the way out, I thanked Bruntford and asked her if it was really horse.

She looked at me and asked, "Why? Do you want to go and tell them it **isn't**?"

WHAAA OO AAAAT?

And she was right, which is always a **surprising** thing to discover about an adult. You know, because of how they are.

ADULTS can be a bit WEIRD

They watch the news even though it makes them angry.

They watch sports even though it makes them angry.

They have kids even though they make them angry.

Science has no explanation for ADULTS.

FRIDAY 13

Dear Dumb Diary,

I asked Isabella why she had even wanted to have an arm-wrestling competition in the first place. She said she did the whole thing so that Jake and Emmily could meet and see how much they had in common, like a love for arm wrestling, and thinking that puppets are alive.

It might be hard for other people to believe that Isabella would go to all this trouble for another person (or **any** trouble, for that matter), but I happen to know that Isabella has a soft spot for Emmily. This is evidenced by the several times she has elected not to put the **KICK ME** sign on Emmily's back again after numerous impacts knocked it off.

She likes Emmily so much

that often she hardly even enjoys tripping her.

Saturday 14

Dear Dumb Diary,

Aunt Carol came over today. She was going shopping and asked Angeline to join her and they decided to stop by and see if I felt like going along.

Remember, Dumb Diary, that Aunt Carol is also Angeline's aunt now because she married Angeline's uncle. I know I have explained this to you before, but I want this to serve as a warning to future Jamie to be **very careful** who she marries, and to consider the impact your marriages will have on the environment. Especially the environment of your various relatives, who will have to deal with your husband and his relatives, even though they did not share in the joy of picking out a wedding dress and bossing around your bridesmaids.

Unless he's really handsome. And plays guitar.

And RAises kittens.

then you don't have to consider your relatives.

When Aunt Carol and Angeline invited me to go shopping, I suggested we pick up Isabella. They reminded me that Isabella was currently not welcome at the mall due to a misunderstanding about a bottle of bubble bath liquid and their fountain and somebody who looked like Isabella being videotaped pouring one into the other.

Long story short: That could have been anybody that looked like Isabella, and the fountain needed to be cleaned anyway. And probably the floor. And possibly the pants of the forty people that slipped in it.

So we went without Isabella, because the mall is a **mystical, magical, majestic** place where you may find all of the world's treasures (but make sure you get a receipt, because when you get home you may find that some of the world's treasures make some of your other treasures look fat). And I couldn't pass that up.

The Mirror in The Dressing Room

The Mirror in my Bedroom

We went to a bunch of stores and watched Aunt Carol almost buy a tremendously ugly purse, but we sneered at it so hard she dropped it like it was full of scorpions. (**Oldsters**, we will always be there for you, telling you when things are gross, if you just call out to us.)

We had lunch at the mall, too. For some reason, food always tastes better when it's surrounded by stuff you can't afford.

And then two amazing things happened **at the same time**: First, I saw Hudson Rivers with his dad across the mall and he **guy-waved** at us.

HOW GUYS WAVE

① ② ③

OR, IF THEY ARE REALLY WAY INTO WAVING...

① ② ③

The second thing was that Chip, who is the **number one** cutest guy in our school, walked over and asked Angeline if she would meet him at the Fun Fair.

Chip is cute enough to be in a commercial for men's cologne, but he is not that kind of weird cute where you can tell he would be just as cute if he had been born a girl. Chip also has a **supercoolness** that never quits.

Angeline did not choke on the lemonade she was drinking and then start laughing out of some kind of weird embarrassment — which I may have done, but that is a perfectly normal reaction when you are unexpectedly avalanched by that much coolness.

Instead, Angeline barely smiled and quietly said, **"I guess."**

Hi Chip.
Heh heh heh
heh heh
heh heh
heh heh
heh heh
Hi Chip.
Heh Heh

Hi. Heh heh
heh heh heh
heh heh HEH
HEH HEH
Hi Chip.
Heh heh heh
heh heh, Hi. heh

And that's when my **superpowers** kicked in. Hudson was watching us from across the food court, and his face just fell. And then a split second of anger flashed across it, and then a microsecond of sadness. And then he turned, and was gone.

Don't think I'm nuts here, Dumb Diary, but I believe it's possible that boys, like ants, may actually, really, and truly **feel things**.

Other Things Boys have in Common with Ants

Both have enormous Abdomens.
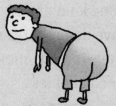

Both are quite comfortable with dirt.

Actually, it may have just been that one boy at the water park with an enormous Abdomen.

74

Sunday 15

Dear Dumb Diary,

Once, there was a **huge wart**. Either it ate something terrible, or it contracted some kind of horrible illness, and a beagle broke out on its skin and began to grow.

When it achieved maximum grossness, the beagle ate the wart and lived on by itself. Eventually, this wartdog came to be known as Stinker, my beagle.

Stinker grew in size and odor, living mostly on dog food, morsels dropped on the floor, an occasional sock or underpant, and for dessert, his own **foul moods**.

In order to anger me as deeply as possible, Stinker married Angeline's dog, Stickybuns, and they had puppies together. One of those, Stinkette, is also my dog.

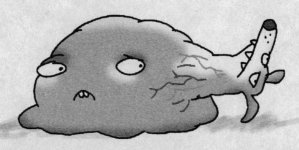

Stinkette inherited many qualities from her dogdaddy. She looks like him, smells putrid like him, and has similar tastes in food, which is why I'm even mentioning this.

This morning I was talking to my ant jar, encouraging the ants to live at least until our report was due, and I noticed Stinkette snurfling under my bed.

When I dragged her out, she had dust bunnies on her nose, and had evidently eaten quite a few because she started making the loud **KACK** noise beagles make to indicate that they have eaten something they didn't care for, and are about to kack it out on the floor.

YOU GET USED TO IT.

The sound of the kacking, and the appearance of the partially swallowed dust bunnies, suddenly reminded me that **I might have to kiss Mike Pinsetti.**

In a panic, I ran downstairs and gathered a bunch of things so I could set up a practice bottle-toss game in my backyard and try to improve.

I set up bottles to tip over with a tennis ball, and a drawing of a clown to **avoid** hitting with the ball, just to be safe. (I don't think I could hospitalize a clown with a tennis ball, but I don't want to take that chance.)

When the dogs saw me go outside with a ball, they assumed that it was for them, because chasing after balls is one of the most important things in the world to dogs, right after scratching, slobbering, and things I'd rather not talk about.

Stinker is a huge **ball hog**, so if Stinkette was going to get any chance at all to play, I had to throw it directly to her. This is harder than you might think, because Stinker likes to use his gargantuan fatness to get between me and Stinkette. If Stinker was just four pounds heavier, the city would make us get a permit to operate a dairy.

Still, I managed to get the ball past the cow-beagle thing, so Stinkette got a chance to play.

After a while, Isabella and Emmily came over for more ant study, and Angeline tagged along because she said she finished her report already and would help with ours if we wanted.

They watched me play with the dogs before I put them inside so that I could demonstrate the fake Fun Fair game I was going to use to practice.

Isabella objected, saying that she made the bet with an unpracticed Jamie, and that practicing this way was cheating.

But both Angeline and Emmily stood up for me, saying practicing was perfectly fair — Angeline pointed out that it was how she learned the guitar, and Emmily pointed out that it was how she learned **pointing**.

And then, just to show Isabella how things worked, I set up the bottles and threw a high-speed, perfectly aimed tennis ball **onto the roof**.

my technique was perfect. Must have been something wrong with the ball.

The next ball was much closer, bouncing off a window behind which Stinkette was frantically trying to catch it.

The following ten throws went a variety of places. I never hit the target, but I was getting closer. Isabella was laughing so hard she wrote, **"Please stop can't breathe"** in the dirt with her finger.

I finally had to stop when my arm started to hurt and my mom came out and said that Stinkette was slobbering all over the glass and I should quit before she peed.

Isabella didn't change her mind about me practicing, but she did ask me to record it next time so she could watch it anytime she was depressed.

We went inside and got to work writing down all sorts of **ant junk**, like that they only live for six to nine weeks, except the queen, who can live for years and have millions of babies. Also that a colony is almost all females, who do all of the hard work, with only a few tiny flying males winging around the queen.

I included in our report that I think it's pretty unfair that girl ants don't have a choice in the things they do. Maybe some of them want to fly, maybe some of them want to strike out on their own and be queens of their own colonies. Maybe there's an ant that just wants to do things **her own way**.

When I said that, I noticed that Angeline wrote it down. She wrote only three words on her paper: **Her Own Way.** She had a faraway look in her eyes, like she was thinking hard about something, or had been very recently kicked in the face.

SO WHAT, ANGELINE, I can have a faraway look, too

I can Look, LIKE, SIX FEET Farther AWAY THAN You

Monday 16

Dear Dumb Diary,

In the cafeteria today, Emmily said that Jake asked her to meet him at the fair and she told him she **couldn't**.

This really surprised all of us, because Emmily will accept an invitation to watch you do laundry.

When we asked her why, she said it was mostly because she had **already met him**. Then she called us stupid for not remembering that she'd met him at the arm-wrestling competition.

Being called stupid by THE STUPID just isn't that insulting.

After a few minutes of explaining her little mistake to her, and how "meet" can mean a couple different things, Angeline told Emmily to just go explain to Jake and tell him that she wanted to *meet up* with him at the fair.

Isabella chimed in that girls can't ask boys to things because **asking is the boy's job.**

Angeline was a little angry at this and asked Isabella if she thought we should behave like a bunch of ants, and follow some set of bug rules about what the females could and could not do.

GIRL ANT
TO-DO LIST
1 WORK
2 DIE
3
4
5
6
7

It turns out that Isabella may have been listening in class after all, because she pointed out that there are a heck of a lot more ants in the world than there are people, so maybe we **SHOULD** take a little advice from the ants, who were at least smart enough to get rid of all the blond-haired ants long ago.

I'm almost friends with Angeline now, but that doesn't mean I'm friends with her hair, and I had to laugh at Isabella's scientific observation.

(I'm afraid our arguing may have confused Emmily, whose eyes cross when this happens. It was probably the comment about **blond ants**.)

Angeline stood up with a look on her face like my mom after Dad makes a **dadmistake** (examples include: "Yes, it makes you look fat" or "Don't worry, we can still eat this"). Maintaining eye contact with Isabella the whole time, she walked over to a table where Pinsetti was sitting and asked him, loud enough for me and Emmily and Isabella and Hudson (who was sitting just a couple tables away) to hear, **if he would like to meet up with her at the Fun Fair.**

Time seemed to stop for a minute, especially for Pinsetti, whose breathing also did. After a little shake, he snapped out of it and said yes.

Angeline walked back, sat down, and said to Emmily: "You see? You can ask Jake if you want to. Anybody can ask anybody."

Emmily nodded, smiled, and said, "Yeah, I know. I just don't want to."

Pinsetti paralyzed by BLONDITIS

While Isabella laughed, I watched Angeline swallow hard, realizing that she had just asked Pinsetti to the fair after she had already told Chip she'd meet him there, and all because she was trying to prove a point to somebody who already understood it.

And I felt sorry for her.

I didn't feel the least bit sorry for Angeline's eyelashes. Not one bit. I'm not friends with those, either.

But I did feel sorry for the girl they were dragging around.

I'm **NOT** friends with **ANY** of her nice qualities

If she was a **BALD**, featureless **TORSO**, we'd probably get along much Better.

Tuesday 17

Dear Dumb Diary,

Today I looked at my jar of ants, which I now realize are all girl ants, and explained to them it wouldn't be much longer before they could go free. I just wanted to turn them in with the report, and then that would be that. I tried to cheer them up with some candy, which I gave to them in very small pieces gently lowered into the jar.

Then I put them on the highest shelf in my room, because I could feel Stinkette's beady little **beagle eyes** glaring at the candy in the jar.

Beagles are GREED at one end

And GENEROSITY at the other

Because I'm a little bit psychic (it comes with the superpowers), I detected some tension between Isabella and Angeline in science class. I think that Angeline may blame Isabella a little for putting her in that position with Pinsetti. Also, the big heart with **"Angeline Loves Pinsetti"** written on it that Isabella made and held up for Angeline to see in class could have contributed to the hard feelings.

Isabella very nearly got caught by Mrs. Maple, who I suspect may use those long, waggling toes to detect things the ways ants use their antennae.

Angeline didn't really react at all, which is the **number one way** to infuriate Isabella. I'm not sure if I told that to Angeline, or if she figured it out by watching TV shows about handling the criminally insane or babies.

The Toe reminded us that our ant reports are due in ten days, and Emmily raised her hand to ask a question.

When Emmily raises her hand, teachers always grit their teeth, take a huge inhale, and then let it out in one big burst through their nostrils. They've learned from experience that there are generally **four categories** of questions Emmily asks:

1. "Can I please go to the bathroom?"
2. "Where is the bathroom?"
3. "Is it okay if I raise my hand and ask a question?"
4. "I don't understand anything you've said in the last thirty minutes. Could you explain it again, please? Also the last six weeks."

But Mrs. Maple called on her anyway.

And Emmily asked, "Why are ants so strong? You don't see other little things, like hamsters, lifting couches over their heads. And if the females are that strong, wouldn't the boy ants be even **better** at doing the work, since boys are stronger than girls?"

Mrs. Maple's mean face was replaced by one of astonishment that Emmily had asked a real question. The rest of us were astonished, too, and we probably would have listened to the answer except for the fact that it was **astonishingly boring.**

Except Isabella listened. And she listened very carefully.

Angeline noticed and made a **"What's up with Isabella"** face at me, and I made a **"Yeah, I know"** face back at her.

I don't know. That face kind of looks like this I guess.

Wednesday 18

Dear Dumb Diary,

So, Isabella said that Emmily had given her an idea. In the same way that Emmily had questions about boys, she figured that other girls at our school might have questions about boys. Using my new superpowers, I could answer them. **For a price.**

The problem was going to be that we needed to conduct the operation so that nobody knew who was answering the questions. We'd need a **partner** to be the face of the operation. To work, this plan would require that we first determine who the absolute brightest girl in the school was.

often you can identify the smart by their glasses

And sometimes their T-shirts

I ♥ my 🧠

And then make sure that she never talked to Emmily, who was going to be our partner.

We laid it out for her like this: She would go around and collect questions, and then she would give them to Isabella, who would ask her brothers for the answers. That's what we told Emmily, anyway. *Really* it would be me answering the questions. (Isabella's brothers wouldn't give her the answers anyway. They wouldn't give her anything better than a bruise.)

Emmily was to charge **one dollar** per question.

which one is the pancake and which is the dollar?

I tested her. She **CAN** do this.

By the end of the day, Emmily had only collected three questions, but it was just the first day. Here they are, along with the answers my superpowers gave me:

A Girl Asks: *Why do boys like to wrestle and fight each other all the time?*
My Superpower Answer: *For boys, winning at fighting is like having the coolest shoes or the best-looking nails.*

AGA: *Why do boys love video games so much more than girls do?*
MSA: *In a boy, violence occupies the same place that loveliness occupies in a girl. Until they program a video game that is operated by loveliness, girls won't like them as much.*

AGA: *Jake is probably the strongest boy in our class. Pound for pound, do you think there are any toothed animals nearby that are stronger?*
MSA:

My superpowers had nothing for this last one. I asked Isabella whose question it was, and she said she couldn't read Emmily's printing. Guess that's one dollar we aren't making off my powers.

Thursday 19

Dear Dumb Diary,

I know that we need a visual aid for our ant report, but I'm beginning to feel guilty about keeping these ants bottled up. It's hard for me to even look them in the eye anymore. **Their kajillion teeny, accusing eyes.**

I saw Hudson at my locker today, looking cute in an **eighthish** sort of way, and he was saying something about the Fun Fair but I wasn't really paying attention because my superpowers told me it was something like, "Would you ask Angeline if she's going to the fair and if she is would she hang out with me unless that would be all weird or **derp derp derp?**"

Really, Hudson, if you have something to ask Angeline, go ask her. Please don't take up my time making me not pay attention to what you're saying. For your information, I have more important things to not pay attention to.

ALSO CURRENTLY NOT PAYING ATTENTION TO:

NEW DEVELOPMENTS IN SHOELACE MANUFACTURING

ENDANGERED ANIMALS THAT ARE MEAN AND GROSS

EYELASH PROBLEMS FACING BEAUTIFUL BLONDS.

Angeline asked us if we were the ones sending Emmily around collecting questions. Since we think of Angeline as **almost** a friend, we told her it was true because Emmily already had.

We told her that Isabella's brothers were giving us the answers. Angeline didn't believe us until Isabella explained that for each answer they give her, her brothers are permitted to expel **one large spit** upon her. Angeline recognized that arrangement as a likely one, and accepted the story.

it's pretty much a standard deal for them

Here are a few more of the questions that Isabella collected from Emmily today:

A Girl Asks: *Why are you handsome boys always jerks?*

My Superpower Answer: *We aren't. You just notice it more when we're handsome because you're so surprised to find that the inside isn't as nice as the outside. It's like biting into a chocolate and discovering a toad inside when you're expecting a delicious cherry. The truth is, anybody can have a toad center, or a cherry center. And there are even poisonous, exploding toad centers, and cherries that are full of more cherries. That's probably why we give girls boxes of assorted chocolates: to remind them of this fact without coming out and saying it, which is something we don't feel comfortable doing about things.*

AGA: *Emmily, who is putting you up to this? Is it Isabella? Or Jamie? Stop writing that down. I'm not really asking a question.*

MSA: *Okay. We know that Angeline asked that and I already answered her. (Technically, she owes us a buck.)*

AGA: *Look, I need to know. Is there anybody around stronger than Jake? You don't know me.*

MSA: *I have been getting a lot of questions from different girls about Jake, so you should know you aren't the only girl who's interested in him. I think he's the strongest boy in our school, but I feel that you really should consider some other qualities. For example, you might like a boy whose neck is **not** as big around as his head.*

Boy Necks are available in a variety of diameters

Friday 20

Dear Dumb Diary,

Today I saw Isabella talking to Jake, and she offered him a piece of gum. This is pretty significant because Isabella has a **relationship** with gum. No matter how hard she gnaws it, the gum doesn't bite her back, and she loves it for that. I always thought of gum as a boy that Isabella was dating — ten to twenty minutes at a time.

But not anymore. When I saw Jake take that piece of bubble gum, I knew that **she** had been the one asking those questions about him.

Only love would make her share gum. Only love would make her clap while he blew a big bubble. Only love would make her pop it so hard that she poked her finger almost down his throat.

Okay. Maybe the poking part is difficult to interpret. But Isabella is new to this. She's just opening her heart to the possibility of love and almost making somebody gag in the hall.

When she saw me watching, she wiped the gum off her finger onto his shirt and walked quickly away.

She's such a flirt.

I've decided not to question Isabella too much about this, for two reasons:

One, I'm afraid that if I embarrass her, I might injure the fragile, delicate part of her heart that is exploring love for the first time. **Two,** she might injure the fragile, delicate part of my heart that is pumping my blood.

And she could do it while bathing a porcupine.

Saturday 21

Dear Dumb Diary,

I started bright and early with the bottle-toss practice today, which means I spent forty-five minutes throwing the balls to Stinkette in the yard while Stinker went nuts trying to get them first. Stinker tries hard to get the ball, because he's naturally **greedy** and **demanding** by nature, but he is also **old** and **tubby** by nature, and I kept throwing it into Stinkette's mouth every time.

Eventually, Stinker tipped over in slow motion, like a statue of a much larger, solid concrete beagle. Then Angeline jumped over the fence and into the yard, because I guess she had been watching me for a while.

FAINTING FROTH

"It's really not nice to spy on people," I said.

"It's really not nice to give your beagle a heart attack," she said back.

I informed her that he didn't have a heart attack. He just faints like that when he's mad that he's not getting his way.

"Look," I said, sticking my pinkie in Stinker's nostril. Instantly, he was up and on his feet and sneezing all over the place. "I think it's his **reset button**, I don't know. Anyway, it stops him from faking. Try it on your dog or grandma if you think they're faking."

Angeline said she had come over to help me practice for the bottle toss. I couldn't ask Isabella, and Emmily wasn't much help — every time I missed, I had to spend, like, ten minutes cheering her up.

So I accepted Angeline's offer, even though I still believe there was some **spying** going on.

I think I should teach Doctors my amazing technique

I didn't manage to knock over any bottles, but I did get very close one time — although at the actual fair, I doubt that Angeline will let me bounce it off her that way.

Angeline asked me about Hudson, and if I knew who he wanted to meet up with. I said **of course** I knew. (**Duh.** He makes it pretty clear. I guess she was just checking to see if it bothered me that my probable future husband was in love with her.)

She was surprised when I told her that Isabella is deeply in love with Jake, so it would be nice if she wouldn't be attractive around him until he falls in love with Isabella and then she can do her blond thing again.

It may sound like there is still a small amount of envy there, but like I said before, I really don't hate Angeline anymore. We're **practically friends**, although I can't imagine it would kill her to slouch around Hudson and have bad breath.

It's something I would do for a friend.

if Angeline was REALLY my friend

she'd try to look like THIS all the time

Sunday 22

Dear Dumb Diary,

Emmily called today and said that she had more questions, but they were all from her dad, who asked them just to be nice so we could make a few dollars. I told her that I guessed that would be okay and she read me his questions:

Emmily's Dad, Pretending to Be a Girl, Asks: *Why is Emmily so sweet?*
My Superpower Answer: *Uh. I don't know, Mr. Emmily's Dad. She just is.*

ED, PTBAG, A: *Isn't Emmily so very pretty?*
MSA: *Very pretty. We all like Emmily, but these aren't real questions.*

ED, PTBAG, A: *Emmily is like a princess. Don't you agree?*
MSA: *Tell Emmily to give you your three bucks back.*

I'm starting to think that I'm not going to be able to use my superpowers to make money. This is probably why superheroes all have normal identities, so they can actually make a living.

HOW SUPERHEROES MAKE MONEY

Spider-Man knits sweaters.

Superman screws the lids on pickle jars.

Iron Man, as you would suspect, just irons.

Monday 23

Dear Dumb Diary,

    Of all the people in the world, it was **Isabella** that talked Emmily into asking Jake to meet her at the fair.

    It went something like this: Isabella walked up to Jake and told him that Emmily thought it would be really cool if they hung out at the fair, and since Emmily's dad was working the concession booth, he'd give Jake all the popcorn he wanted.

    Emmily was very surprised to hear that her dad was working the concession booth since he was going to be out of town that whole week, and Isabella explained that it was a **surprise** so she shouldn't ask him or anybody in authority about it.

AAAGH!

WHY IS IT SO DARK?

Emmily is also a little surprised by nighttime.

EVERY DAY.

A lie, of course, and a pretty beautiful one considering that Isabella has been in love with Jake for weeks. It is beyond me why she would — **OH. MY. GOSH. IN. CAPITAL. LETTERS.**

Again, Isabella just amazes me. Isabella, in spite of her feelings for Jake, is stepping aside and bringing him and Emmily together, because she knows that it is their destiny.

I wish I could tell her what a beautiful, sensitive, loving soul she has, but I'm certain it would get me punched in the neck.

people. PEOPLE. PLEASE. Let's keep important things in **CAPITAL LETTERS.**

danger.
huge
baby-eating
scorpions ahead.

Tuesday 24

Dear Dumb Diary,

Lots of the ants have died, and I decided to leave the jar open outside and let the living ones go free. I don't really want to turn in a jar of **dead ants** with our homework, but if we don't use them now, they will have died for nothing. I'm afraid that much drama would force me to write a play about them.

A scene from my play

I watched Isabella watch Jake at lunch today. As I did, I noticed that Hudson was watching me watch her, and Angeline was watching him watch me, and Emmily was watching the corn on her plate.

My superpowers told me that Hudson is **crazy** about Angeline, and Isabella is **crazy** about Jake, and Emmily is **crazy**. My superpowers are truly becoming stronger and soon, I'm sure I will understand why males want to watch sports so much.

When I got home, the jar just had dead ants inside. I suspect that the living ones saw that the lid was open and **made a break for it**. They didn't even take the Cap'n Crunch with them.

When word of this gets back to the rest of the ant community, I'll bet the **ant scientists** that are working on how to avoid getting stepped on by five-year-olds will also be working on a way to avoid giant blonds coming at them with jars.

Wednesday 25

Dear Dumb Diary,

I finished our ant report today. I included everything, even the part about letting the living ones go free. I'm still not an ant fan, but I hate them less now. I think I understand them better.

Emmily would not shut up about learning to **glitterize**, so I gave her just the cover of the report, after I outlined the title. I explained exactly how to put the glue down and shake the glitter onto it, and I'm pretty sure she'll be fine.

I asked Emmily if she wanted to decorate the dead ant jar as well. Maybe it won't be as depressing if she adds a little **bling**.

I asked her to keep it, you know, dignified

DEADSY WEADSY

Hudson called after dinner, but I didn't call him back since I know he was just going to ask me questions about Angeline and her beauty and her personality and all of that stuff. Nothing against Hudson, but he really has to come up with **better things** for me to assume he wants to talk about.

I didn't need to LISTEN to HUDSON. MY POWERS told me what he would have SAID....

Angeline Angeline Angeline Angeline ANGELINE Angeline Angeline Angeline ANGELINE

Aren't. Super. Powers. Just. Great.

Thursday 26

Dear Dumb Diary,

Isabella saved a life today.
Let me explain.

At lunch, she wanted to sit at the table where Jake and Emmily were eating, so she dragged me along. Isabella sat down right next to Jake. (She's still a little in love.) Emmily was sitting right across from him.

Isabella was staring so intently at Jake that he clearly started to get uncomfortable. I wasn't sure he was even going to finish his third serving of meat loaf, or horse meat, as he now believes it to be.

Every once in a while, Emmily would say something totally **Emmilish**, like, "Why don't they grow more foods on the cob? That's the most fun way to eat corn. They should put everything on cobs." Then Jake would laugh, of course, because that's all you can do when Emmily says something like that: You either laugh or suggest she gets some tests.

One of the times Jake laughed, he started to cough a little, and that's when Isabella saved his life. **By sticking her finger in his mouth.**

I've had Isabella's finger in my mouth many times. Whenever I yawn, Isabella loves to quickly stick her finger in my mouth to disrupt it in mid-yawn. Isabella is also not above reaching into your mouth for gum if it's your last piece and you just put it in there.

But as familiar as I am with her finger in my mouth, I have to tell you, you never really get used to it.

And for Jake, **this was a first**.

I learned at a young age that just because it's in your mouth Isabella doesn't believe that it's necessarily yours

He sputtered and coughed harder and sprayed Emmily with what was essentially aerosol meat loaf. He could only remove Isabella's finger after several minutes of intense struggle, because it seemed as though she intended to keep it in there for good, and Isabella is pretty strong.

When he finally got it out, Isabella announced that he was okay, and that she had succeeded in poking the lump that was choking him to death down his throat.

I started clapping, since **lifesaving** is a pretty magnificent thing to do. But Jake wasn't thanking her, and Emmily looked pretty upset.

"You didn't tell me he was going to blow food all over me!" she said to Isabella, and she looked as though she might cry. **"Did he even bite you?"** she added.

This is the point where Isabella clapped her hand over Emmily's mouth and led her out of the cafeteria, with me following close behind.

"Bite you?" I said. And I was going to ask why she would want him to bite her, and then it all became clear.

The bite.

"You thought if he bit you that you would get **boypowers**, didn't you?" I peered at Isabella. "And you just wanted Emmily and Jake to spend time together so you could get close enough to make your move."

Isabella always tells the truth. Every time. Every time you catch her in a lie, she tells the truth. If she can't get away with lying more, she tells the truth.

"He was really jumpy after the bubble-gum thing," she said. "What else could I do?"

THE PLAN IN ACTION

MUNCH

step 1.   step 2.

Isabella said it was my fault because I **cheated** by practicing the bottle toss. She figured that if Jake bit her, she might get powers the way I got them from Fat Ricky, and then it would be a fair bet again. The basketball game and the arm wrestling were to help her determine who was the most powerful boy, and whose bite would do her the most good.

Then she whispered, "I was afraid I was turning into a girly girl, because we hang around with Angeline more now. I was afraid that whatever she has is contagious, and maybe **that** was how you kicked me in the face."

I was flattered that Isabella respects me enough to cheat so badly, and with such little regard for others.

Only a **true friend** could resent me that much.

the people that resent you

REALLY understand you

Friday 27

Dear Dumb Diary,

Today we handed in our ant reports. Emmily ran in late with the finished report cover (she forgot where the classroom was again), stapled it to the report, and put it on Mrs. Maple's desk. I think we did a good job. I hope so anyway.

I didn't see the ant jar, and I asked Emmily where the dead ants were.

"They're in a better place," she said.

Such a sweet sentiment. I smiled. She probably gave them an adorable, stupid little funeral.

They use some of the classrooms for the Fun Fair. This year, they're using Mrs. Maple's class for the bottle toss, where I'm afraid things are going to go badly for me and my lips, **Pinsetti-wise**.

When class was almost over, Mrs. Maple asked some of the boys to help move her desk to get ready for the fair. Emmily stood up and said girls are strong, too, and in the ant colonies the girls do all of the hard work, so why can't girls help her move it?

Teachers are always shocked when they discover that you've learned something, and are even more shocked when you actually apply it somehow to the real world. Plus, this was **Emmily** who said it, and realizing that Emmily had learned something could make a teacher's entire career. Mrs. Maple *had* to say okay.

Isabella and I stood up to help. I guess we were obligated to, since we were Emmily's report partners. Plus, I think Isabella might have been trying to make up for the events of the last couple weeks.

we're like sister ants working together
to lift a sugar cube or Barbie Desk.

Mrs. Maple got on one side of the desk, and we got on the other three sides and lifted it.

As we were huffing and puffing, I said it would be easier to just slide it, and Isabella agreed, and we all dropped the desk before Mrs. Maple had a chance to share her opinion. Now that I think about it, her opinion might have been something like, "Okay, just let me get my **mutant toes** out of the way before you do."

But she didn't, and we didn't, and the next thing you know, she was screaming and we were lifting the desk off her finger toes and she was flopping down in her chair.

Mrs. Maple was angry and in pain and making those grunting sounds that adults make when there are kids around and they can't shout the swear words they crave.

I knelt down and examined her toes to see if they looked broken.

Then she suddenly stopped grunting, and I figured she had died from **toe pain**. But she was staring at the cover of our report that was sitting on her desk. She was squinting and turning her head back and forth the way beagles and dads do when they're trying to understand something.

And then I realized why.

It was **Emmily's glitter job**.

When she got home with our report, Emmily discovered that she didn't have any glitter to complete the cover. She had glue, but no glitter.

But she did have a bottle of dead ants.

That's right. Emmily had used the **ants for glitter**.

Mrs. Maple's recovery was nothing short of a miracle. She started laughing, and then getting creeped out, and then laughing again. She limped out of the room and we heard her walk down to the next teacher's room.

After a minute, we heard them both **explode** with laughter. Mrs. Maple came back with tears in her eyes.

"Grossest — and most amazing — visual aid I've ever seen," she said, and started laughing some more.

I apologized for dropping the desk on her, and she said, "Oh, I'm okay. With these **weird toes of mine** it happens all the time. I'm surprised you haven't noticed them before."

We all said no, no, we hadn't noticed them, and they look perfectly normal to us, and they're **just regular toes**, and all that stuff.

Except Emmily, who said she noticed them all the time and wasn't surprised that we dropped the desk on them.

And Mrs. Maple laughed even harder.

Emmily can't help saying what she thinks.

Yes, It _does_ make you look fat. Maybe even extra fat.

Excuse me, Mr. President, we just heard you fart.

I have 19 pairs of underpants and they're all named Suzy.

Saturday 28

Dear Dumb Diary,

TODAY WAS THE FUN FAIR.
And I was terrified.

Aunt Carol drove me and Angeline over to the school this morning. They could probably detect that I was slightly nervous by the way I was **trembling violently.**

I didn't want to tell them, but I had to get it off my chest. Even though they were an adult and a gorgeous person, Aunt Carol is okay for a grown-up, and Angeline is less detestable to me now than she used to be.

As we pulled into the parking lot, I couldn't wait any longer. "I'm going to have to kiss Pinsetti, and even my superpowers can't save me."

They looked at each other and Aunt Carol silently parked the car. Then they turned around and asked in one voice, **"WHAT superpowers?"**

I explained everything. How I acquired my powers through a boy bite, how I kicked Isabella with them and used them to sense boyfeelings. They listened quietly and sympathetically about each and every stage of my transformation and nodded thoughtfully.

And then Aunt Carol **lost it**. I mean, she laughed so hard she choked on her gum. At the time, I thought I might have caused the chokage with *other* superpowers of mine, because I was really happy about how well it shut her up.

How FUNNY would it be to Mentally choke the critical

After Aunt Carol managed to swallow the gum (remaining in her stomach now for seven years, which **serves her right**), she and Angeline gave me their opinions.

First, Aunt Carol said, you don't get superpowers from being bitten by a boy, or a spider, or anything else. And if those kinds of superpowers really existed, we wouldn't have oil leaks or earthquakes or anything like that. Our superheroes would save the day all the time, and clearly there are days that just don't get saved.

BITES FROM THESE ANIMALS WILL NOT GIVE YOU POWERS

And Angeline said that *she* understands how boys think. Not all boys, and not all the time, but sometimes. Even though she doesn't have superpowers at all.

And then I said that if they were right, how was it that I understood all boys all the time, and how could I flawlessly answer questions about them?

Angeline said it was because I'm just good at observations. I watch people carefully. I listen to them.

"Besides," Angeline said finally, "you don't understand *all* boys."

I nodded. "If you mean understanding why all guys like to watch sports and no girls do, I'm working on that one."

I have not ruled out the possibility that they are simply morons.

Aunt Carol started laughing again, so hard that I offered her another piece of gum to choke on. "What are you talking about?" she howled. "I love watching basketball. And I kind of like baseball sometimes, too. Dan likes football, but he would rather watch a movie than baseball or basketball."

"I like watching football," Angeline said. "Although my dad doesn't. He does like hockey, but only when his team is winning."

This, frankly, was a lot to absorb. These were two of the **girliest girls** I knew, but they liked some of the **boyiest things** there are. Evidently, sports aren't just a boy thing. Some girls like watching some sports. Some boys don't.

Is it possible that human beings aren't just like ants?

But they had forgotten something. I'd kicked Isabella. In the face. I asked them to explain how I managed **that**.

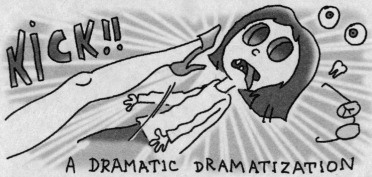

A DRAMATIC DRAMATIZATION

"You're fast, Jamie," Aunt Carol said, waving her arms around. "Plus, Isabella probably didn't expect it. Maybe it was dumb luck. Maybe Isabella just isn't that tough."

Angeline put her hand on Aunt Carol's shoulder. "No. **Not that last one.** You're wrong about that last one," she said quietly. "Isabella is that tough. It was more likely dumb luck. Really dumb. The dumbest."

I spent a long time saying good-bye to Aunt Carol, since I was in no mood to go to the bottle toss without my superpowers. Finally, she pried my hands apart and wriggled free from my farewell hug and Angeline and I went in to the Fun Fair together.

Isabella has asked to do this for her birthday every year since she was four.

Isabella found us right away, of course, because more than anything on earth, she was really looking forward to **making me look like a dope** at the bottle toss.

We ran into Hudson inside and he asked me where Chip was, and I said I had no idea.

"But you're meeting up with him here," he said.

"No, I'm not. Angeline's meeting up with him."

"No, she's not. Angeline is hanging out with Mike Pinsetti today. Everybody heard about that. Besides, I saw Chip ask you at the mall."

"No, no," I explained, "he was asking Angeline."

Then Angeline walked up behind me with Pinsetti. "Nope, I'm hanging around with Mike today," she said, and she pointed down the hall.

Before I could even process what I was seeing, Angeline leaned in and whispered, "I asked Chip to stick with her, and honestly, I've never seen him happier."

She was right. **Emmily was walking along with Chip**, cutest boy in our class, and she was making him grin and laugh the way she does it to us. He just couldn't stay supercool around her. **Emmily had Kryptonited his cool.**

Then I looked at Hudson, and he said something I'll never forget until somebody says something better to me. "I was hoping you'd want to hang around at the fair, but then I thought you were hanging around with Chip, but I never see you guys talking, like ever, and I thought maybe something had changed, so I've been trying to say something about it for weeks."

What? **HE. HAD. WANTED. TO. HANG. AROUND. WITH. ME.** I hadn't sensed it. Not at **all**. Not one bit.

HUDSON'S INTENSE CRUSH RAYS

DOINK

So I don't have superpowers. Aunt Carol was right, and Angeline was right. **HUDSON** was the boy Angeline was talking about in the car. He was right up there in my face, liking me, and I hadn't picked up a thing.

Isabella was listening, and suddenly she also knew that I didn't have superpowers.

"Let's go try out the ol' bottle toss," she said, yanking me along to my doom.

"You coming?" I said to Hudson, and he smiled.

off to meet my DOOM...

I was really not looking forward to having Isabella make me look like an idiot, or make me pay up with Pinsetti, in front of **everybody**.

I was sweating and my stomach hurt and I was a little wobbly.

"You go first," Angeline said, and she pushed me up to the front of the line where the guy handed me three balls and explained that I had three tosses to knock over all the bottles. Right. Like the explanation was going to help.

Angeline said, "Wait."

But I threw the first ball, and it bounced off the chalkboard and landed in the back of the room. I picked up the second ball.

Angeline said, "Wait."

I threw, and the ball bounced off the ceiling and into the wastebasket.

Only one more ball before my fate would be sealed. I could hear my lips softly weeping.

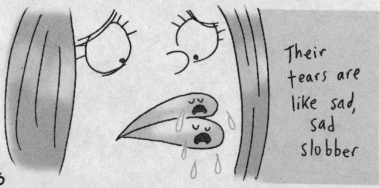

Their tears are like sad, sad slobber

But Angeline said, "Wait," and grabbed my arm.

"Don't throw it at the bottles. You're not a **thrower-atter**. Think about how you throw the ball *to* Stinkette. You're a **thrower-toer**. Do it your own way."

She was right.

I threw the third ball *to* the bottles, and knocked two of the three of them over. Not enough for a prize, but nothing to be embarrassed about.

SMASH!

Isabella was shocked.

She was shocked, but not intimidated. She took her place as Angeline leaned in and said something to the man running the booth, just as he was preparing to hand Isabella the balls. He went pale in the face, grabbed a stuffed pink koala, and handed it to Isabella.

"Game's over. You win a prize. Who's next?"

The kids in line behind us jostled Isabella out of line as she started to complain, "Wait a second! I didn't get to throw."

The guy at the booth shook his head. "You already won a prize. The limit is one prize to a player. Those are the rules, Jamie."

"Jamie?" Isabella said.

"Jamie?" I echoed.

As we walked out of the room, Angeline grinned at Isabella in such a way that made it clear that it had been **her** who had foiled Isabella's plan.

"Why did that guy call her Jamie?" Hudson asked.

Angeline smiled. "I told him that Isabella was Jamie Kelly."

"So?" I asked. "Why would that win her a prize?"

Isabella answered for her. "Because all of the guys running the games know about you and **Dart Number Three**. They're probably friends with that clown, Beepo — maybe they visited him the hospital, or drove him to his physical therapy."

Isabella scowled at Angeline, but I think I saw a faint, respectful smile **wriggling around** underneath it.

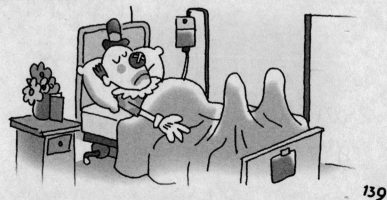

Angeline was totally nice to Pinsetti for the rest of the day, and it never seemed weird or **boyfriendy-girlfriendy**. It was just normal, and Pinsetti wasn't even all that gross.

Chip and Emmily laughed and laughed so much that they had us all going.

Later on, Jake joined our little group, and he couldn't take his eyes off Isabella. Who could blame him? She's a wonderful human being and is probably the only one in the school that could keep her finger in his mouth for a full minute.

And Hudson and I had a lot of fun, too, even though I kept feeling dumb that I had thought superpowers were real.

They're not.

sorry, guys

Or are they? I mean, how does Angeline just make people feel comfortable around her? And why does everybody like Emmily, no matter how goofy she is? She uncooled Chip and cured Mrs. Maple.

Maybe I don't **always** know what boys are feeling, but lots of times I know what they're feeling. And ants. And aunts, too.

I mean, I *did* knock down two bottles, once I understood what **my way** was. And in a time of dire emergency, I heroically touched antenna-like finger toes. I **am** good at observing things, and I guess I can naturally speak the male language.

Okay, so maybe I do have superpowers.

Maybe we all do.

We just have to find them.

Thanks for listening, Dumb Diary,

Jamie Kelly

P.S. Oh, one more thing — Isabella's superpower. Remember how Isabella has a soft spot for Emmily? And since it turns out that Chip is not better at those games than I am, Isabella gave Emmily the koala bear she won at the bottle toss.

And the unicorn she won at the ring toss.

And the alligator she won at the basket throw.

Isabella gave Emmily **all twelve** of the prizes she won.

You probably think that Isabella's superpower is winning games, but it's not.

Isabella just walked up to each game and introduced herself as Jamie Kelly.

That may sound like her superpower is her cleverness, and that's part of it, but when you think about it, Isabella's real superpower is that she's friends with me.

What's YOUR Superpower?

Check off all that apply!

- [ ] Glitterizing
- [ ] Observing
- [ ] Winning games
- [ ] Listening
- [ ] Flying
- [ ] Making people laugh
- [ ] Not getting grossed out by super-gross things
- [ ] Invisibility
- [ ] Extreme coolness
- [ ] Understanding others
- [ ] Leaping tall buildings
- [ ] Excessive cuteness
- [ ] Inner beauty
- [ ] Genius brain
- [ ] Superspeed
- [ ] Homework-finishing

Being awesome is only half the battle.

Dear Dumb Diary,

A long time ago, I wrote a letter to the president about the space program and how it would be a good idea for **ME** to select the people who should be shot into space.

I made a lot of very good points about who should be selected, such as weight, ease of stuffing into a bag and tossing into a rocket, unnatural blondness of hair, and how much happier our Earth would be as a result. I was much younger when I wrote it, and I understand that my ideas would not have been seriously considered.

But that was six months ago, and now I think I am **qualified** to choose.

POISON APPLE BOOKS

POISON APPLE™

The Dead End

This Totally Bites!

Miss Fortune

Now You See Me...

Midnight Howl

Her Evil Twin

Curiosity Killed the Cat

At First Bite

THRILLING.
BONE-CHILLING.
THESE BOOKS
HAVE BITE!

#1: Let's Pretend This Never Happened

#2: My Pants Are Haunted!

#3: Am I the Princess or the Frog?

#4: Never Do Anything, Ever

#5: Can Adults Become Human?

#6: The Problem With Here Is That It's Where I'm From

#7: Never Underestimate Your Dumbness

#8: It's Not My Fault I Know Everything

#9: That's What Friends <u>Aren't</u> For

#10: The Worst Things In Life Are Also Free

#11: Okay, So Maybe I Do Have Superpowers

#12: Me! (Just Like You, Only Better)

Danny Shine just wants to draw comics, buy comics, and talk about comics. But first, he has to get his name off of

THE LOSER LIST